FORESTS

BIOMES OF NORTH AMERICA

Lynn M. Stone

Rourke
Publishing LLC
Vero Beach, Florida 32964

www.rourkepublishing.com

PHOTO CREDITS: All photos © Lynn M. Stone

Title page: *The Douglas squirrel lives in the rich, damp forests of the Northwest.*

Editor: Frank Sloan

Cover and interior design by Nicola Stratford

Library of Congress Cataloging-in-Publication Data

Stone, Lynn M.
Forests / Lynn M. Stone.
     p. cm. — (Biomes of North America)
Summary: Looks at trees that make up the world's forests, animals that dwell in them, and how forests are changing.
Includes bibliographical references and index.
  ISBN 1-58952-684-8 (hardcover)
  1. Forest ecology—Juvenile literature. 2. Forests and forestry—Juvenile literature. [1. Forest ecology. 2. Forests and forestry. 3. Ecology.] I. Title. II. Series: Stone, Lynn M. Biomes of North America.
  QH541.5.F6S768 2003
  577.3—dc21
                                                         2003004370

Printed in the USA

CG/CG

Table of Contents

Arctic Circle
Canada
United States
Mexico
Cuba
North American Forest
0
1500 KM
0
1000 Miles
Forest

The Forest

A forest is hard to see, someone said, because it has so many trees. And that is exactly what a natural forest is: many trees growing over a large area. The trees grow close enough together to form a roof, or canopy.

Many kinds of forests grow in North America. Each type of forest is made up of different kinds of trees. Some forests are made up of needle-leaved trees, like pines and spruce. These forests are called **coniferous**, because the trees bear cone fruits.

Deciduous forests are made up of trees with "broad" leaves, such as maples and oaks. Deciduous trees shed their leaves each autumn.

Woodlands with a mixture of deciduous and coniferous trees are called mixed forests.

Snow coats a coniferous forest of spruce trees in Jasper National Park, Alberta.

Tropical rain forests grow in the warmest, wettest parts of North America. Temperate rain forests grow in wet, but cooler, regions, like parts of Alaska and Washington.

Many reasons, soil for example, explain the growth of one kind of tree instead of another. **Climate** plays a large part, too. Most deciduous trees, for example, will not survive extreme cold.

A wolf hides behind a screen of deciduous maple leaves in autumn.

Forest Communities

Each forest type is a community of a variety of plants and animals. In one way or another, these living things depend upon each other for survival. Within the community, each plant and animal has a special habitat, or home.

The plants and animals of one forest community type are largely different than those in another.

The lynx lives in the coniferous forests of the North. Its cousin the bobcat lives in many kinds of wetlands and woodlands, but not in the coniferous forest.

The forest trees provide insects and nesting holes for the red-headed woodpecker.

Many kinds of plants in addition to trees grow in the forests. Some types of forests have far more plants than others. The plants are food for animals, large and small. In turn, some of the plant-eating animals become **prey** for meat-eating animals, the **predators**.

When forest creatures die, their bodies rot and make the soil richer. That soil gives birth to new plants. In this way, a forest community continues to renew itself.

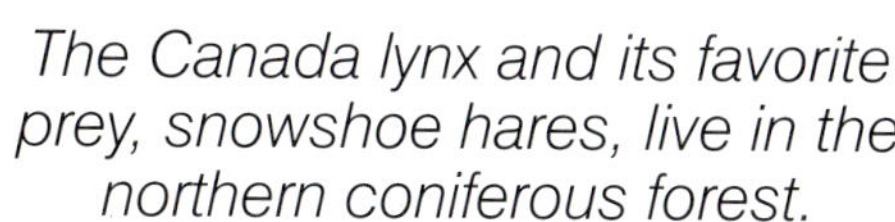

The Canada lynx and its favorite prey, snowshoe hares, live in the northern coniferous forest.

13

Forest Animals

Animals live throughout the forest, from the forest floor to the canopy. Some, like certain squirrels, owls, woodpeckers, insects, snakes, and rodents, spend their entire lives in the forest.

Others, such as whitetail deer, toads, black bears, raccoons, and wild turkeys, are part-time forest animals. For them, the forest is a good place to hide or find food.

A forest oak offers a meal of acorns to a whitetail deer, one of many acorn eaters.

Forest creatures have many ways of living
there successfully and more or less safely. Some,
like tree squirrels and martens, are expert climbers.
Deer fawns can't climb, but they have **camouflage**.
Lying still, they blend into the brown, leafy
forest floor.

Walking-stick insects survive with another type of
camouflage, called **mimicry**. A mimic looks like
something else. The walking-stick looks like—you
guessed it—a stick!

*The walking-stick insect
mimics a forest twig!*

The Changing Forest

Over long periods of time, forest trees grow, age, and die. But they don't usually die all at once. So the forest, while always changing, remains a healthy community of plants and animals.

Changes that people bring to forests, however, are rarely healthy. Some of the greatest old forests in North America have been cut down and replanted with fast-growing trees of only one kind.

Natural events like wind, lightning fires, and the seasons change forests naturally.

Snow whitens a mixed forest of spruce and aspen trees in the Colorado Rockies.

The prevention of natural forest fires has hurt many forests, too. Most natural fires burn quickly. They don't destroy the forest. Instead, they kill weeds and leave healthful **ash** behind. They also keep forest **litter** from piling up.

Forests that never have natural fires become full of dry branches and leaves. When a fire does strike, it has all the old litter to burn. It grows too hot. Such fires destroy forests.

The fire in this Florida pine forest has been set to burn up forest litter and keep the forest healthy.

Great Smoky Mountain National Park in Tennessee and North Carolina is just one national park that preserves North American forests.

Glossary

ash (ASH) — burned pieces that are left after a fire

camouflage (KAM uh flazh) — a pattern of colors or shapes that allow an animal to blend into its surroundings

climate (KLY muht) — the weather of an area over a long period of time

coniferous (cah NIFF uh ress) — trees that normally have needle-shaped leaves and produce cone fruits, such as pine trees

deciduous (dih SIJ uh wus) — trees that drop their leaves more or less at the same time each year

litter (LIT tuhr) — twigs, leaves, bark, and other plant material that piles up over time on the forest floor

mimicry (MIM uh KREE) — in nature, the close similarity of one living thing's appearance to another's, even animal to plant

predators (PRED uh turz) — animals that kill other animals for food

prey (PRAY) — an animal that is killed by another animal for food

INDEX

Further Reading

Johnson, Rebecca L. *A Walk in the Deciduous Forest*. Carolrhoda Books, 2001
Nadeau, Issac. *Food Chains in a Forest Habitat*. Rosen, 2002
Nelson, Julie. *Forest*. Steadwell Books, 2001
Staub, Frank. *America's Forests*. Lerner, 1998

Websites To Visit

www.efn.org/~dharmika/overview.htm
www.yahooligans.com/Science_and_Nature

About The Author

Lynn Stone is a talented natural history photographer and writer. Lynn, a former teacher, travels worldwide to photograph wildlife in their natural habitat. He has more than 500 children's books to his credit.